Frankenstein, 1931.
Sci-Fi Movie Posters: 6 Cards
© 2019 Dover Publications, Inc.

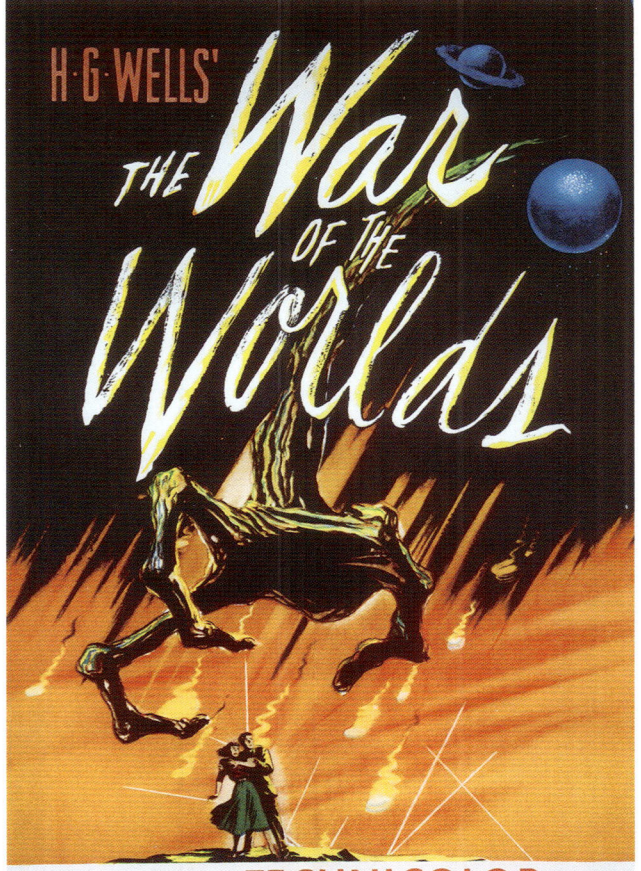

The War of the Worlds; 1953.
Sci-Fi Movie Posters: 6 Cards
© 2019 Dover Publications, Inc.

The Invisible Man; 1933.
Sci-Fi Movie Posters: 6 Cards
© 2019 Dover Publications, Inc.

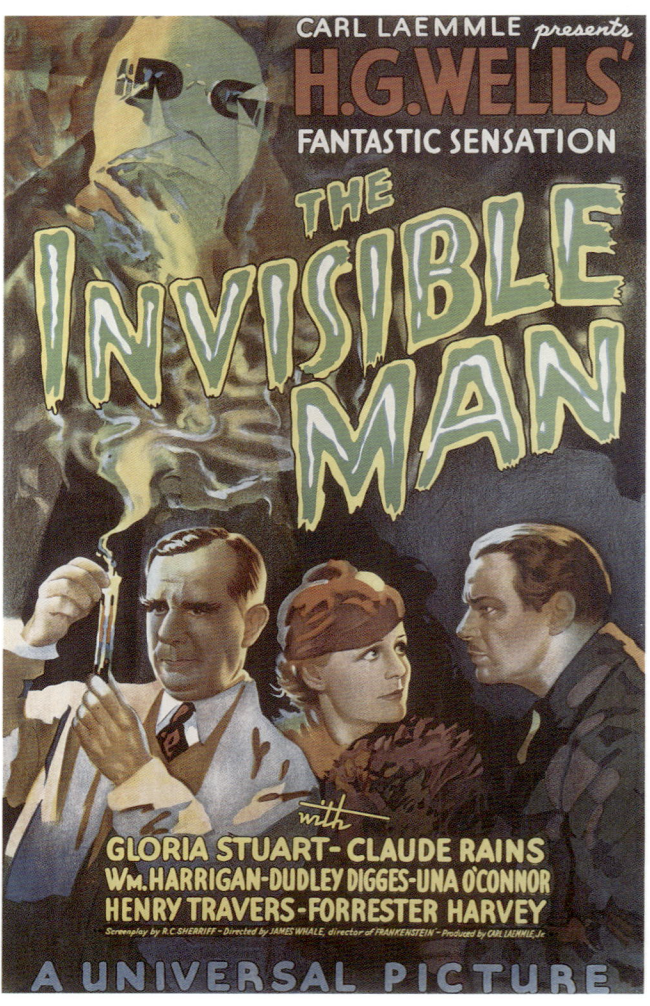

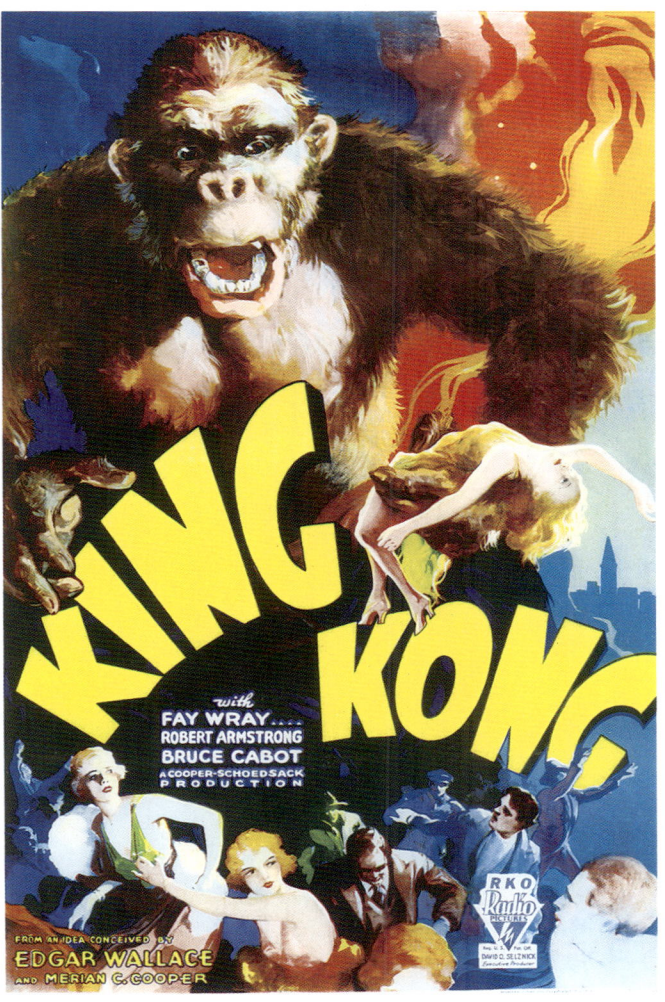

King Kong; 1933.
Sci-Fi Movie Posters: 6 Cards
© 2019 Dover Publications, Inc.

Dracula, 1931.
Sci-Fi Movie Posters: 6 Cards
© 2019 Dover Publications, Inc.

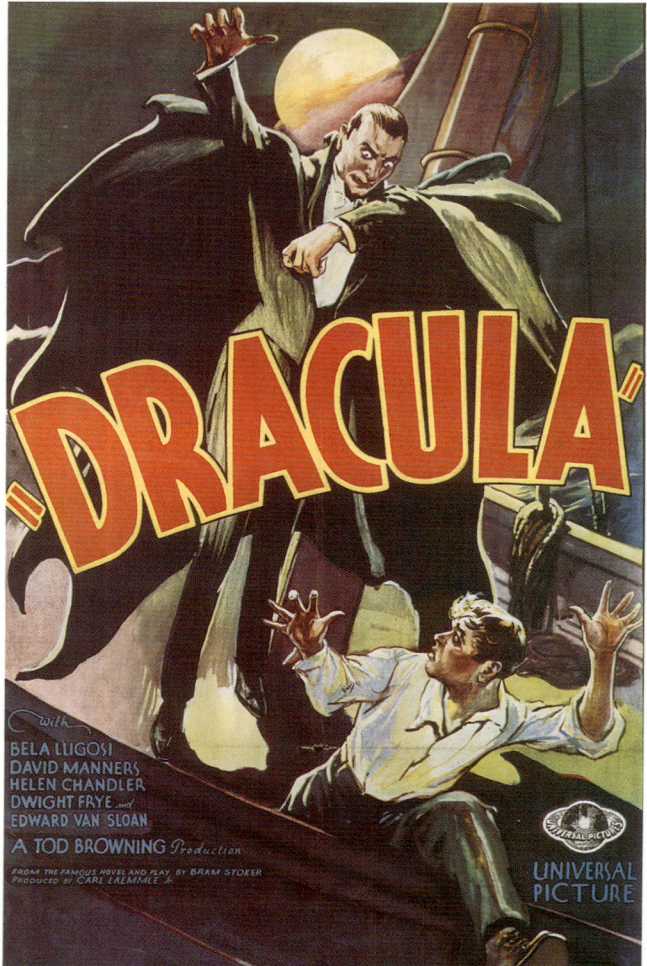

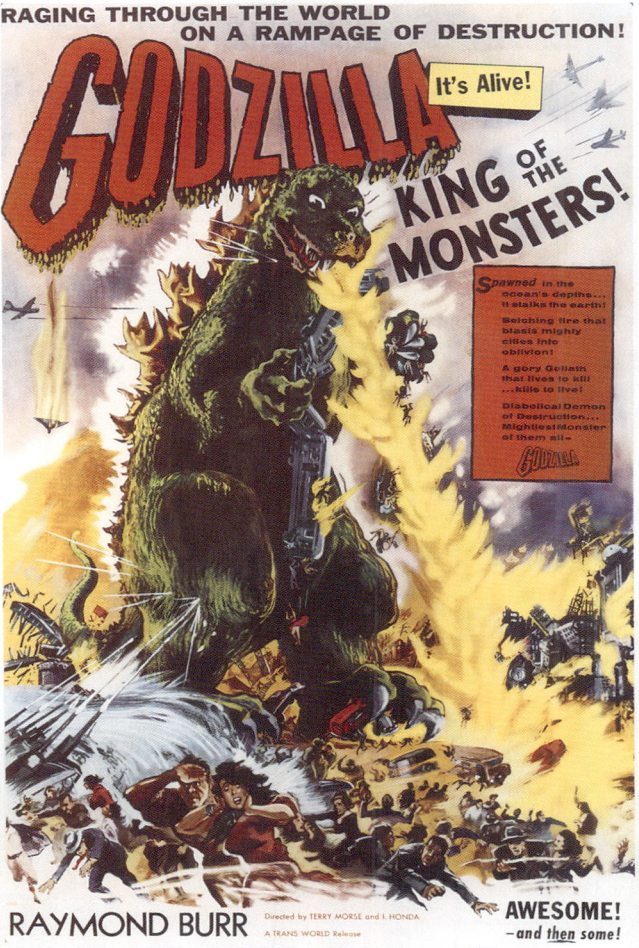

Godzilla, King of the Monsters!, 1956.
Sci-Fi Movie Posters: 6 Cards
© 2019 Dover Publications, Inc.